Help! I'VE LOST MY LLAMA

by Colette Warbrook

illustrated by Mark Wilcox

HELP! I'VE LOST MY LLAMA

ISBN: 978-1539670001

www.thewritinghub.co.uk

www.artbywilf.co.uk

For Ewan

Tim lives on a farm.

His parents have lots of chickens, a few pigs...

...and also llamas!

The llamas are very funny.

And they don't spit as much as people think they do...
just don't steal their food!

Tim even has his own llama, called Lottie.

They've been best friends since they were babies.

He feeds Lottie and takes her for walks.

And they especially love playing football.

Tomorrow Tim starts school for the first time.

"Mum! Can Lottie come to school, *pleeeeease*?" he asks.

"I'm sorry, Tim, but llamas aren't allowed in school. They're not housetrained and they don't like sitting still in class."

"*Hmmmm*. We'll see about that," thinks Tim.

So, he comes up with a *VERY* clever plan to take
Lottie to school.

But not in his mum's car...

...in his tractor.

Tim has a small, red toy tractor. It has an engine but isn't very fast.

"I'm sure it will get Lottie to school... at least by lunchtime," he says to himself.

The next morning he tiptoes into Lottie's barn and whispers his plan in her ear.

Lottie carries on munching her hay while Tim talks. He hopes she is paying attention.

OPERATION GET LOTTIE TO SCHOOL
1. Put Lottie in tractor
2. Give her a map
3. Meet at lunch
4. Play together
5. Meet Mum
6. Go home

"Breakfast!" Mum calls.

"I'm on my way," says Tim. "*Now Lottie, listen carefully. I'll be back to get you ready just before I leave, OK?*"

Lottie carries on eating her hay.

After breakfast, Mum helps Tim put on his new uniform.

It's itchy and much too big. He feels ridiculous.

"I'll get the car," says Mum.

It's time for Tim and Lottie to put their plan into action.

Tim runs back to Lottie's barn and drags his tractor out from its hiding place.

It's a bit of a squash to squeeze her in. But Tim tells her she doesn't have to drive far.

That's the next problem...

...llamas can't drive.

Tim quickly shows Lottie how to drive a toy tractor.

He turns on the engine. It splutters...

...but soon tractor and llama are making their way out of the back of the barn.

"Tim, where are you?"

"Sorry, Mum," Tim puffs, as he runs outside.

As they drive out of the gate, Mum looks in her car mirror.

"That's odd," she says. "Is that Lottie following us in your toy tractor?"

"Don't be silly, Mum. You know llamas can't drive."

"Oh, of course. Silly me."

"*Phew!*" Tim thinks. "That was close."

Tim's mum gives him a hug at the classroom door.

But he can't see Lottie.

At lunchtime he eats fish fingers with mashed potatoes and peas, followed by jelly and custard.

He then goes outside to play with his new friends.

Tim is having so much fun that he forgets about Lottie.

Later, Tim looks around the playground but there is still no sign of his llama.

At the end of school, his mum arrives.

He's starting to get worried, so he tells her about
Operation Get Lottie To School.

"Oh dear, Tim. Don't worry, we'll find her."

Back home, they look in the barn...

...the pigsty...

...and even ask the chickens if they've seen Lottie.

"Quick! Look at this!" Dad shouts from inside the house.

Tim and his mum rush indoors.

On the TV is a llama, lying on a beach towel at the seaside, next to a toy tractor.

"Breaking news! Families at Starfish Sands were in for a surprise today. They discovered that llamas can drive tractors and they also love to sunbathe. Back to the studio..."

That evening, Tim gets ready for bed and waits for Lottie to come home.

He then hears a loud noise coming from outside.

"BEEP! BEEP! Chugger, chugger, chugger..."

He looks out of the window.

There's his toy tractor... and Lottie!

Tim's mum reads Tim and Lottie a bedtime story.

And just this once, she lets Tim eat an ice cream right before bedtime.

After all, Lottie has brought it all the way back from the seaside.

And Tim doesn't even mind that it's melted...

...just a little bit.

The End

Printed in Great Britain
by Amazon